A Battleaxe and a Metal Arm 2:

Kneel Before Zhug

Samuel Fleming

Cover Art by David Leahey

ISBN-13: 978-1-954679-05-4 (paperback)
ISBN-13: 978-1-954679-04-7 (ebook)

Thank you to my Beta Readers

and to my First Reader,

Mel.

Contents

"The first death is not the hardest.
Neither is the second."

—*forgotten*

Previously...

The elven spellweaver, Helesys Byyra, and her human barbarian comrade, Taunauk, found themselves in an underground room with no memory of how they got there and no discernible way in. The two carefully made their way down the long passageways and came upon an old greatworm tunnel and flooded sections of underground.

Their first encounter was a group of fishmen. It was the first test of their skills, one that Helesys met with a deadly blast from her metal arm and Taunauk with cunning swings of his axe. They learned that the fishmen were not mindless monsters. They were cunning and even had spellweavers among them.

When the water around their knees stilled, the two pressed on through the dark confines of the rusted prison. There they were nearly set upon by a swarm of ghostly black squid, but were saved by a spiny, scaly creature. Pitiful Lull, as Helesys referred to him, was cryptic and interested in the elf's wand-arm. The pair sent the creature scurrying away through the rusted bars. At the edge of the metal confines, they found the first prisoners: A scaled serpent and diseased fishmen, neither of which could be helped.

The pair pressed on, past one huge final cage stretching from ceiling to floor, and snuck past an encampment of hundreds of fishmen. The creatures covered a massive set of stone stairs that lead to a small prayer room. They paid the floating faeries no mind as Helesys solved the puzzle-locked door to the beyond—but not before being discovered by the fishmen. Both Taunauk and Helesys held the barricade and were able to escape through the stone door, destroying the locking mechanism behind them.

Beyond they found an injured water elemental, a whirling, faceless creature. While Helesys convinced it to accept her aid, zombies rose up in the water-logged room. Taunauk held them off while the spellweaver pulled a shining object free of the water elemental. Then with their combined force, they made swift work of the undead threat.

The shining object was an engraved metal plate depicting a wolf, with various geometric edges on the back—which Helesys recognized as a key. They would not have time to use it, as the fishmen found another way into the room and brought a gargantuan hydra with them. The fishmen weavers were able to maintain control of the great beast and, though the adventurers fought nobly, both would ultimately perish: Taunauk in the maw of the creature and Helesys crushed after she destroyed the flooded chamber.

But death was not the end. The pair awoke, again falling to the floor of that very first room. The wolf-plate, somehow still in their possession. The passageways of the dungeon, somehow changed. They were puzzled, but quickly set to purpose:

Escape.

The Abandoned
Barracks

The dungeon had changed when they died.

When they first woke down here without memory, there was only one hallway. Only one way to go.

This time there were two.

The barbarian, Taunauk, led them through the left hallway. He towered over his elven comrade. The shoulders of his fur cloak were silhouetted by the torch he carried, giving the illusion of a sun rising over a mountain. He carried the massive battleaxe in his other hand.

Helesys walked behind the giant human, more or less in darkness as so little light spilled from around his frame. She knew—they knew—little more of each other than their appearance. The elf knew that she was a spellweaver. That her gray robes hid elven chainmail. Beneath, her skin was fair, her muscles strong and supple. She might have been a noble but she could not say for sure.

She knew that her right arm was prosthetic from shoulder to fingertips. It looked like a sleek, armored gauntlet and was indiscernible from such at a glance, but underneath it was a fusing of metal clockwork and arcane power. Embedded in the forearm was a magic wand. It, like the arm, was an extension of herself. She felt every trickling and surge of power. She could call upon it wordlessly and at a moment's notice… If only she could remember how to do so. Her powers, like her memory, were gone. Slow to return.

These questions about her powers and her memories were heaped upon an ever increasing mass of questions. Not just where they were and how they got there. But how they lived again after dying… What had changed about the dungeon and why? And so they were going back in the direction of the flooded temple.

Helesys wondered if the fishmen and the flooded temple would still be there. For if they were there then so was the cold water, the gloom of the rusted prison… so was the hydra.

"I do not think the plate is the cause," the barbarian whispered, his head hidden from view by his mountainous shoulders and fur-lined cloak.

"Nor I," the spellweaver, Helesys, replied. "Maybe if things were the same…"

Though elf could still not remember the specifics of magic, she remembered the larger rules—just as her body recalled how to roll upon falling from a great height and how she called upon the cannon blast of her arm. All magic was governed by rules which meant that it had limitations. If such powerful magic was really contained within the plate, then she should feel its latent magic. Instead, the engraved wolf plate felt mundane. For contrast, her arm felt magical. This *place* itself felt magical… Some ominous mix of wonder and foreboding—something fitting of a place of such power.

Every two dozen paces she turned, weary that something was following them, and found nothing but the endless stone corridor stretching into the black. No matter how many times she looked it did not assuage the nagging feeling of being followed.

The human added, "You called this place a *dungeon*. Why?"

This brought Helesys back. There were the obvious answers: The place was underground. It was dark and lit with torches. In truth, that was where the similarities ended. She could not remember much—anything—of her life before, but she felt innately that most dungeons were small and similar to the rusted prison. They were not sprawling with miles of tunnels and containing forgotten temples and strange civilizations.

Like so many other things, the elf did not know why she used the word, *dungeon*, when referring to this place.

Helesys sighed in frustration as she followed the giant barbarian. "I do not know. Only that I feel like a prisoner. One who has broken free of her restraints and is trying to find a way out."

Taunauk was silent a dozen steps before replying, "Our memories will come back and so will the knowledge of a weaver. Then you will know what this place is."

"I wish I had your confidence."

"You solved the ancient stone puzzle," he added, referring to the water pipes in the temple, "you will solve this as well."

Helesys smiled in the gloom. "You let the burden of the mystery fall upon my shoulders. What is that? Confidence?"

"We each have strengths. Shoulders meant for different things," he added in jest.

"I believe that metaphor is appropriate for precisely one of us. My mind and your brawn."

"Your cunning and your wand. My axe and my sense."

~

Cold stone stretched on and on down the hall. The hallway was ten paces wide and the same high. It stretched on and on for a mile without end. All as it had before.

"We should have seen it by now," Taunauk grumbled. "It was half a mile to the wormsign and we have gone twice that."

Helesys remembered. It was the first thing they had come across—a great gaping hole in the hallway—the old remnants of a great worm's passage through the area. It had swallowed the hallway as it passed perpendicular to the stone, carving a massive tunnel in its path. The passage had been old and and collapsed on either side, but it had been eerie nonetheless. A mark of gargantuan things to come.

"You are right," the elf finally said. "Do you think that spells the same for the flooded temple?"

"It might."

They passed through another mile of empty hallway. Far enough that they should have passed into the start of flooding—had they been going toward the temple of the fishmen. But Helesys was all but certain that they were not. The dungeon had changed and they were now walking blind again.

One other thing was different—the feeling of being followed. Helesys could not shake it—the feeling of eyes staring over her shoulder. Each time she turned back she saw nothing but endless empty hallway.

She could stand it no longer.

"Do not be alarmed," she whispered to her barbarian friend.

Helesys summoned the power of her wand-arm, the cool trickle of power called to a surge. Her entire arm hummed as whirled and leveled her right hand down the hallway, toward the eerie void. She let loose a dark purple blast that filled the hallway and washed through the corridor in a silent scream until it was no more than a pinprick down the hall.

The shot *appeared* to hit nothing and yet that did not make her feel the slightest bit better. Helesys tried to steady her breathing. Was it just another trick of this blasted place?

She turned and saw Taunauk, axe in his hands and torch on the floor. The fire cast sharp shadows on the wrinkles of his face.

"Anything?" he asked, his eyes searching the black.

"No. Nothing I can see."

"You were wise. Never ignore a feeling." After a few moments, Taunauk picked up the torch and continued onward. Every two dozen steps, he turned back as well.

~

Instead of flooding or a temple, they came to a dozen rooms that lined the hall. Taunauk stopped and smothered the torch with his cloak before setting it down in the now dim light of the hall. He slowed to a prowl as they approached the first set of rooms—the first sign of anything but themselves. The dozen rooms were paired and evenly spaced, each set twenty paces from the next.

Taunauk hugged the wall and peered into the left room and then the right. Helesys kept her eyes down the hall.

"Anything?" she whispered.

Taunauk motioned for her to follow him as he slipped into the right room. The elf stepped into the room behind him, almost unaware that her wand-arm had been vibrating with anticipation. She kept watch over the hall and glanced Taunauk's direction as he checked the room.

Inside, the room was little bigger than the hallway. Wooden frames and scraps were heaped in the corners, stacked as high as Taunauk. Metal lockboxes were stacked around the piles, holding them to form. Taunauk carefully opened the lid of one box and found nothing. He checked one more before turning away. The musty smell of the hallway faded only slightly, replaced by the rust of lockboxes and scrap metal.

"Nothing," Taunauk mumbled and motioned for her to follow him again. The pair stepped back into the dim hallway and pressed further.

Helesys peered into the left room, the one that Taunauk had skipped and saw more piles. This time of armor pieces, each piece broken or pierced or bent. The elf stepped inside to examine the pile and saw several pieces with the same design: Three heads of a wolf. The middle facing forward and either side facing outward. It would've been a simple thing to discount had she not the wolf plate in her robe pocket.

The elf weaver pulled out the silver plate and compared it with a scrap piece of armor. The three-wolf design of the armor was an obvious mirror of the wolf-plate—the right-facing wolf of the armor was an exact match of the plate they found in the flooded temple. The only difference in style was the make: The stamped lines of the plate were clean and crisp compared to the forged lines on the armor.

She had so many blasted questions already! Her own mysteries plagued her, but now it seemed as if the dungeon had a depth of facets as well. It had been tempting to think of the dungeon as a swirl of randomness and chaos, but it obviously was not: The wolf design popping up in two different dungeon instances flew in the face of that idea. What was the connection between wolves and the dungeon? What else carried over between instances… between deaths? Were those old places lost to them?

"*Stercus*," she mumbled. Even the meaning of the elvish curse was lost on her.

She slipped the wolf-plate back into its pocket and the scrap piece of armor with the design into another pocket of her robe. Then she walked quickly after Taunauk, who had not paused for her.

They stalked down the hall to the next set of rooms. In the left room, were more wooden scraps, piled high in the corners and kept there by a waist-high ring of lockboxes. In the right room were piles of broken furniture; tables and chairs with legs removed, all piled in the back of the room.

"What happened here?" Helesys wondered aloud. She suspected they would find more trash and scraps in the other rooms as well.

"Mysteries upon our shoulders," Taunauk replied. "*Something* has been here recently." The barbarian glanced twice with his eyes to the pile of broken furniture, drawing her attention toward it.

Helesys noticed the slightest movement in the shadows of the furniture pile. Something small.

The elf stepped to the side of the room, her arm vibrating slightly. It was ready, though she felt she wouldn't need it.

"Do not be afraid," Helesys said quietly as she stooped down. "We are passersthrough and mean you no harm." No sound or motion, but the weaver did not move. A long minute passed before the thing in the pile moved again.

Bloodshot eyes peered back and a small Terran figure half-emerged from hiding, maybe half as tall as Helesys. It's skin was a mix of faint greens and yellows, and covered in patches of black hair. Thin with wiry muscle and knobby bones. Its face was the same lumpy shape with pronounced ridges. Several teeth stuck out slightly over its lips, and black and gray hair framed its head.

"Do not be afraid," the elf repeated. "My name is Helesys. His name is Taunauk."

The creature answered quickly, "I am Widewill. Why are you here?"

Helesys stood and caused Widewill to flinch. She ignored it and kept speaking, "It is a strange thing, but we do not know. We do not remember how we got here. Can you tell us where we are or where this passage leads?"

"This is Widewill's home." The creature came out from its hiding place, wearing a loincloth and crouched-walked across the floor, resting on all fours like an ape. It peaked carefully around the corner of the hallway before speaking again.

"That way leads to the other goblins. To my tribe. To Zhug."

Taunauk grunted. "What are you and the creature saying?" The barbarian was leaning against the wall, a look of impatience on his face.

"You can plainly hear—"

"I cannot." The human gestured to the elf's wand-arm, which was glowing a gentle white beneath the arm of her robe. "I saw the same glow when you spoke to the water elemental. I did not realize then. It is translating for you and the creature."

Helesys turned to Widewill, who had wandered back toward his pile. "Widewill, can you understand my friend?" The goblin shook his head.

"Interesting," the elf said, regarding her arm. That was good that she could do more than destroy. Such things were easy.

Widewill noticed her arm was well. "Are you a weaver? Few understand Goblin tongue."

There was the word again. Helesys searched her memory but found nothing about goblins. She turned to Taunauk. "What do you remember of goblins?"

"Little."

"I can see that."

Taunauk shook his head. "No. I remember little of them: Terrans. Live in large groups… Crafty," he added, eyeing Widewill.

Helesys ignored the human. "I am a weaver. That is why I can understand you, Widewill, but I remember little else about myself."

The goblin shrunk ever so slightly further behind its pile. "Weavers are not to be trusted."

"Who told you that?"

"Zhug says."

"Is Zhug the leader of your tribe?" she asked.

Widewill nodded quickly. "Zhug is lord. Zhug is *God*... Everyone knows that." The goblin's eyes were wide with wonder when he said the words.

"Widewill, we must go that way to leave this place..."

The goblin shook his head violently, "You must not."

"Why?"

"Zhug will not let you pass. Other goblins will not let you. They follow Zhug. They listen to him."

The barbarian asked, "What did you say to upset the little one?"

Helesys shook her head. "He says the other goblins will not let us pass. They follow the god, Zhug."

Taunauk sighed, arms folded over his massive chest. "We will pass by or we will go through. We have little choice."

The elf turned back to Widewill, "We must go that way."

Widewill started to say something and paused several times. Finally, "We are crafty. There are traps."

"We would do better with a guide."

Widewill shook his head. "Cannot go back. Exiled by Zhug."

This puzzled the elf and she thought a moment before asking, "Does one goblin speak for Zhug or does Zhug speak through a single goblin?"

The lone goblin shook his head. "No. There is Stizzai. She is biggest, strongest, but she is not Zhug. Zhug is stronger, is smarter. His shoulders scrape the ceiling. His feet shake the stone."

Helesys said nothing in reply. Whatever their *god* was... It was not a god. The elf felt this as fact within her. Some small flame of remembrance told her that gods did not visit the mortal realm… But more so that gods did not find themselves trapped within a cursed dungeon such as this.

Terrans did. Foolish Terrans such as them.

The elf sighed and turned to the human. Taunauk had been watching the hallway, since he could not follow their conversation.

"We must pass through. Widewill will not guide us," she said. "Also, I do not believe Zhug is really a god."

Taunauk nodded thoughtfully. "All the better for us."

"There is a problem. Zhug is bigger than you."

"Bigger than the hydra?"

She looked at the confines of the hall and the room and tried to imagine some hulking goblin hunched over in its confines. Such a creature was easily twelve paces tall. Formidable—yet nowhere near the size of the hydra.

Helesys shook her head in response to his question. "No. Maybe twice your size."

He grunted in affirmation. "Manageable." Taunauk turned his attention back toward the hall. "We should move."

She turned to Widewill again. "Thank you for your help. We are leaving."

"Wait," the timid goblin said. "The others are crafty—even more than Widewill. Do not go into the Crypt. No matter what they say."

"What's in the crypt?"

"Death," he whispered.

Helesys smiled warmly. "Thank you for the warning, Widewill." Before she turned to go she again felt compelled to say the parting words, "May you wander forever and may everywhere be your home."

The goblin held up a hand as if to say something, but tucked down small again as if to silently ponder the words. Words that Helesys could remember not the origin.

The barbarian and the elf weaver left Widewill and journeyed silently deeper into the dungeon, into the unknown, fully expecting never to see the lone goblin again.

~

As Taunauk and Helesys snuck deeper into the dungeon. The long hallway drug on this time without rooms. They saw no other signs of life, except that they came across traps set by Widewill. The barbarian saw most of these and pointed to them with a stern finger as he passed so that weaver could avoid them. Tripwires and slime covered bricks. Without him Helesys would have no doubt stumbled on a half dozen of them. Thankfully none of them were lethal.

But Taunauk did not see them all.

Thrice he tripped on shifting bricks. They were hard to spot—by then the brick had already shifted under his foot. Any other man might've toppled against the wall, but Taunauk shifted his feet and caught himself, merely cursing the trap under his breath.

Widewill followed some distance behind, cursing each time the barbarian faltered. The goblin stopped to reset the traps as he followed. Helesys simply chuckled at the mirror of the two.

The last hundred section passed uneventfully, with no evidence of traps and the two came to three-way fork in the hallway. They could continue on or go either left or right.

Sconces lined the hall in all directions and gloom gave way to torchlight. Helesys turned to ask Widewill's opinion, but the goblin was nowhere to be found.

"He turned back," she whispered to Taunauk.

"Good. I grew tired of his traps."

"You may have more. He likely turned back because we are near his tribe."

He grunted in reply. "Which way?"

The elf could see no difference between the passageways. "Either is as good as any. Just not to the crypt."

"The goblin said that?"

'Yes. It said Death waited down there."

"I suspect a great many deaths await us," the barbarian replied. "We will make them wait a little longer."

~ ~ ~

The Hallway

Taunauk led them left at the fork and deeper into the torch-filled hall. The ceiling rose and curved another two paces in height. For the first time, Helesys breathed easier, as if the extra room in the hall had lifted a weight from her chest. ...If only for a time.

First it was the traps, mostly trip wires that Taunauk easily spied despite their being nearly-invisible to Helesys. Then strings of broken glass that hung from the ceiling: The glass stopped at head-height, but the string continued to the floor, pooling haphazardly. Half a dozen traps littered the hall, causing the two to navigate a weaving path through them.

"A sound trap," the barbarian whispered. "They are close."

Then there were rooms. They were equally matched on either side of the hall and appeared to be evenly spaced again, though the rooms were twice as far apart and stretched on through the impossible hall.

They came upon the first room. Taunauk peered inside and paused. With his left hand he held up five giant fingers then three, then peered into the room on the right. He held up five fingers again and then three.

They stalked forward and only then did Helesys see what the barbarian was telling her. Inside the left room were rows of bunks. There were three beds in each stack and five stacks arranged around the vaulted room. Laying on each packed-straw bed was a goblin. They slept with no blankets, with their armor half-on and other pieces scattered on the floor. Tiny heads and feet were visible on the top-most bunks, the same faint green and yellow skin and black, patchy fur as Widewill. Short swords, daggers, bows and quivers lay scattered around the room, the scene of disarray reminding her of the glass sound-traps.

Helesys turned and saw the same scene repeated in the op-posite room. All fifteen bunks were full—the elf had foolishly thought Taunauk's hand signal meant there were eight in each room. It was a miscalculation she would remember next time.

Still they pressed onward down the hall—a misstep away from waking thirty goblins.

As they stalked forward, she was reminded of that cursed feeling of being followed. The feeling of eyes over her shoul-der. Yet when Helesys looked back she saw nothing but an empty hallway with scattered traps.

The feeling had been pushed from her mind for a time when more pressing things called her attention, like speaking with Widewill or navigating the traps of the hall, but it never completely went away. It was like an ever-present quiet music, one she could only hear the words of when she was still. It was even more troubling here because the threat of being spotted was very real and the mix of careful concern bordered on par-anoia.

They passed two more sets of bunk rooms, the scene mir-rored in each. Ninety goblins between the six rooms. All the while the traps never stopped. The feeling of being watched never stopped. Helesys scanned the stones of the hall, thinking that maybe goblin eyes were watching them through holes in the walls, but the stones were immaculate.

Sneaking through the hall was painfully slow. A hundred paces after the last bunk room brought them to a hard corner as the hallway turned to the right. Taunauk carefully peered around the corner.

"There is another bend up ahead," he whispered, then gestured with his hand to make a Z-shape.

"Good place for an ambush," Helesys replied.

The barbarian shrugged. There was little choice in the matter. Trying to sneak back past the ninety sleeping goblins was likely more dangerous.

"I will go first," he said. "Wait here."

Helesys felt eyes over her shoulder again, something watching. Something there and yet invisible. Intangible. She looked back over her shoulder and up and, for a moment, thought she saw something standing above her—a single floating eye nearly brushing the ceiling of the hall. She blinked and the image was gone, and the elf questioned whether she had seen anything at all.

Helesys alternated between watching her partner stalk the hall, which might've been another hundred paces to the next bend, and keeping watch on the hall of sleeping goblins. Her heart was beating in her throat. The arcane hum of her gauntlet was a small comfort.

Taunauk was halfway down the hall when he stopped cold and stood straight. He stepped to his left, flush with the stone wall so that Helesys could see.

Six goblins stood at the far end. They were all the same small, hunched build as Widewill, except that these goblins wore haphazard armor. Their shoulder pauldrons and leg grieves were oversized, like they had been made for a man— or stolen from one. Helesys's mind wandered back to the piles of broken armor and wondered how they had come to pass. The goblins also brandished swords and shields and those in the back held bows, already drawn.

Helesys and Taunauk had made no sounds and their whispers should not have alerted goblins hiding around a corner such as they. Somehow they had known. Somehow they had been watching the elf and the human.

The goblin in the front stood tall, like a human or elf. Its muscles were thick and stocky compared to the wiry muscles of the others. Its teeth had grown out to tusks. The elf remembered what Widewill said about Stizzai—the biggest and strongest goblin—and guessed this was her. She wore a full set of armor, even the cap of a helmet. And her armor fit.

The goblin leader walked forward, carrying a spiked mace in each hand.

"You are not welcome here," Stizzai said, emphasizing each word in a gravelly voice.

"We must pass," Taunauk said quietly.

"No."

The barbarian looked confused for a moment before replying, "You speak the common tongue..."

"I speak for Zhug. It is Zhug's will."

Helesys slipped around the corner so she was in the same stretch of hallway. Stizzai and her goblins took notice.

"Ask Zhug if we may pass peacefully. We want nothing and mean you no harm," the elf said.

Stizzai stared at Helesys with bloodshot eyes. "Zhug says you may not pass."

"How did you find us?" Helesys asked, changing the subject.

The goblin leader smiled, bearing her tusks in full, menacing glory. "Zhug sees all. Zhug hears all."

Behind her, the goblins all smiled and repeated quietly, "Zhug sees all." They bounced with quiet excitement as they spoke.

Stizzai leapt at Taunauk with cat-like speed, both maces raised overhead, ready to crash down on him, but Taunauk was ready. The barbarian blocked both maces with the long hilt of his battleaxe—it was no clang of steel, but the impact echoed down the halls. The goblins at the end cheered and let loose their arrows wildly and they struck at the stone behind Helesys.

Down the long hall, Helesys heard the stirring of beds, the clank of armor and the grumble of ninety goblins waking.

Her wand-arm crackled with life and violence. The memory of the wand's gruesome aftermath of the fishmen and one of the hydra's heads popped into her mind. She felt a sting of pity; the goblins would suffer greatly at her hand.

Beyond the pity was the simple fact that Helesys did not know the limits of her power. So far she had fired only singular blasts, the larger of which had left her strained and in agony. Such spells would be useless against the goblins—numerous and able to dodge and duck behind cover. She would need repeating fire or spreadblasts.

Out of the corner of her eye, the elf watched the duel of Taunauk and Stizzai. The goblin leader dictated the battle. She crouched low, fighting with the stance of a goblin rather than standing tall as she had initially. She walked on all fours, using her knuckles while still holding the maces.

But Taunauk was no stranger to this. Though Stizzai seemed even faster than the barbarian, he too crouched low and made himself small. He attacked with both the blades and with the butt of the handle. But even with this new technique, the barbarian's steps were backward and rarely forward.

Several more arrows flew from Stizzai's goblins at the end of the Z-shape hall but they passed harmlessly overhead. Helesys realized that the barbarian had shrunk low to avoid them, to force the goblins to shoot past their leader if they hoped to hit him—something they would clearly not do. So far the fear of their leader was greater than their fear of the intruders.

Helesys knelt and Stizzai's goblins disappeared completely from view behind the crouched and still-enormous frame of Taunauk.

Down the long hall the first of the waking goblins peered out into the hallway. Helesys called upon her wand-arm and purple power crackled around her fingertips. She fired a single small blast down the hall which flooded the stone with churning purple light. It passed harmlessly, quietly, but it caused the goblins to duck back into their bunk rooms. For a moment.

While Taunauk kept Stizzai at bay to her left, more goblins peeked out into the hall. Her arm churned with power and the weaver commanded it to fire a volley of four shots. Her arm stuttered with release, the repeated recoil catching her off guard. Each blast sent a jolt through the metal arm and shoulder, and the elf slid back on her feet.

Two goblins were caught in the blast, their yellow-green torsos pulverized as they peaked out into the hall, disappearing in a cloud of red blood and purple energy. The last two shots scorched the hallway, seeming to hug the surface of the stones like a drop of purple oil sliding down the hallway into the black beyond. Her last shot—wide and high from the recoil—scorched the ceiling.

Helesys groaned in frustration—it was like she was relearning her own cursed body!

It took only moments for more goblin faces to peer around the corner, this time with bows and arrows, and returned her volley. Helesys slipped around the corner as the arrows passed by and bounced sharply off the stone.

She stayed low as more arrows flew over the ducked heads of Taunauk and Stizzai, still locked in their deadly duel. The elf stood, hugged the wall and sighted Stizzai's goblins at the end of the Z-shaped hall. Her arm churned with a torrent and she commanded it to fire another burst of shots—she widened her stance and braced her gauntlet with her mundane hand.

This time she waited for an opening past Taunauk and Stizzai and fired down the short hallway. Four shots whizzed past the two fighters and tore through half of Stizzai's guards, splattering chunks of gore against the wall. The remaining half shouted and ducked around the corner of the hall. Stizzai noticed too, locking eyes with Helesys, even as she whirled in a frenzy of maces against Taunauk. The goblin leader was not surprised like her subordinates.

The elf turned back toward the long hall and was greeted immediately with arrows. She only saw the hall briefly, but goblins were advancing. She leaned back behind cover as the first flew past and knocked against the stone. The arrows came steadily now, the archers trying to prevent her from firing, providing cover for their advancing comrades. There were a dozen goblins running toward her in the long hall—who knew how many archers behind them.

Lightning crackled between her fingers and Helesys stuck her metal arm around the corner and fired a blind spreadblast down the hall. A second later, she heard goblin cries and the squelch of death. The arrows paused.

A part of her, a small part at that moment, felt sorrow for the goblins. But this was a whisper to the hum of arcane energy in her arm and the soldier's training that moved her limbs without thought. It was a whisper against an easy answer of violence.

The woman that would fight one hundred while Taunauk fought one.

She turned past the brawling warriors and fired again, catching the bravest of Stizzai's goblin's in the blast as they turned the corner.

In a battle haze, the weaver turned back to the long hallway and fired again before the archers could regroup. Three more obliterated.

"Look out!" Taunauk roared.

Helesys turned just in time to slip the spikes of a mace. Stizzai had managed to clamber past the barbarian—one mace was still embedded in his hide cloak and a foot was planted on his shoulder as the goblin leader leapt over him.

The elf ducked to the side, careful not to stumble out into full view of the long hall and the renewed volley of arrows. Stizzai descended on her in a fury and Helesys scrambled to stay away from her maces.

Her wand-arm churned with power and as she leveled it at the goblin leader, Stizzai knocked it away with her mace. Helesys felt the dull sensation, but nothing in the realm of pain. Meanwhile, the off-target blast blast erupted down the long hall and the approaching goblins yelled in surprise—a happy accident that Helesys had no time to contemplate. She could only hope it gave the advancing goblins reason to pause.

In a scramble, Helesys fired twice more at the goblin leader, but she spun violently and both shots glanced off the side of her armor, flaring in yellow-white blasts. Helesys dodged a mace by a hair's breadth.

The same soldier's training that guided the weaver's shots told her now to get away. Helesys was out of her element and her opponent's armor was bolstered by magic. If by some luck Helesys could land a direct shot, there was no guarantee it would stop Stizzai.

Taunauk was upon them and Helesys slipped around him in a dance that again placed the barbarian between her and the vicious leader. Just in time for Helesys to fire a haphazard volley of blasts at Stizzai's goblins as they peeked around the corner. Another brave goblin fell to it while they others cowered.

Helesys sprinted down the Z-shaped hall—right toward the remnants of Stizzai's goblins. There was no other way out than through them and through them she would go. The elf weaver's heart pounded as she neared the corner, gauntlet already leveled and ready.

Three bows peeked around the corner, in an attempt to shoot blindly at her. Arcane violence exploded from her hand and if the goblins had any time to shoot arrows then Helesys could not tell for the purple sloshing torrent obliterated everything in front of her. The blast hit the corner and the wall behind it in a crackling explosion, overshadowed by goblin cries of pain.

Stizzai's group of goblins was sprawled out. Three were missing arms—the archers—and were bleeding out quietly. The others writhed in slow, pitiful motions, half-conscious from the blast. The shock of the sight didn't register. Her muscles burned and her metal arm tingled from exertion.

She looked down the hall—toward salvation—and saw the hallway give way to a bright open room behind. She gave no thought to what lay beyond for anything had to be better than the rage of ninety goblins bearing down on them.

"Taunauk," she cried. "We must move!"

Helesys turned back toward Taunauk and Stizzai, and saw both figures running toward her. The goblin leader had gotten past Taunauk again and was dashing toward Helesys with incredible speed, making the barbarian's inhuman speed look like a invalid. Her tusks bared in a roaring fury.

The elf weaver met Stizzai's rage with her own cry of desperation, metal arm crackling with power. She was afraid of the leader reaching her. Afraid that a blast wouldn't phase her armor. Even more afraid of what an accidental blast from her arm would mean for Taunauk.

Stizzai hurled a mace and the spiked tip soured true, clanging against Helesys's metal arm and knocking it away. The blast went high and wide, exploding against the corner of the hallway between Stizzai and Taunauk. The mace landed in the sprawled mess of goblins.

The barbarian cried out in pain. The goblin leader hadn't missed a stride and was upon her in a half-second.

Stizzai swung wildly in her rage and that rage was both Helesys's doom and her salvation. The elf weaver backed away, stumbling and felt the cold stone against her back. She blocked a swing of the mace with her metal arm and felt the vibration ring through to her shoulder. Stizzai's swings were wide and telegraphed, but with such force and ferocity that the elf's breath caught in her throat.

Helesys barely blocked another swing, the vibration rang through her chest. Something inside her knew that her mithral arm would stand up to much abuse, but the rest of her body would give out. The impact of the blow sent her reeling— straight into the corner of the hall—the corner that would be her death if she was caught there.

Helesys rolled to her right, but was cut short by a mace that clanged off the stone beside her. The goblin leader would not let her leave so easily.

So the elf charged her wand-arm and when Stizzai swung to deflect the blast, Helesys kicked at Stizzai's leg to knock the goblin off balance. The goblin lurched and brought both arms up to block the arcane blast. Again the leader's armor caused the blast to glance off—Stizzai was knocked upward, only to spin in a shower of yellow-white and land back on her feet— all before Helesys could fully stand.

Stizzai leapt and brought the mace overhead slamming into Helesys's metal arm with such force that the impact rattled her collarbone and chest. The blow brought the elf back to her knees and crumpled against the stone.

The mace was already overhead again, the vision of the spikes and Stizzai's mad, charred, tusked smile would be the last thing the elf saw.

But Taunauk crashed into the goblin leader from behind, shoulder-tackling her into the stone. The horrific crunch of metal and bone was so loud that Helesys thought the stone itself had broken. The barbarian turned with Stizzai in hand and hurled the stunned leader down the length of the hall—back the way they came.

A dozen goblins, the first of the mass of ninety, rounded the corner and were bowled over by the hurled body of their leader.

The barbarian turned to Helesys and offered her a hand. Blood speckled his face and the shoulders of his cloak. "We must move."

Helesys needed no invitation. She fired two quick blasts down the Z-shaped hall, toward the stunned goblin leader and the fumbling goblins. Purple energy tore down the hall but she didn't watch to see if they struck true. The elf and the barbarian sprinted down the end of the hall and—hopefully—toward some measure of salvation.

~

All her thoughts fell away, except that of running as fast as she could. Their feet pounded on the stone and seconds drug on. The cadence of desperate breaths and steps.

Then they emerged into the room and stopped—surrounded by two hundred goblins. Bloodshot eyes and tusked smiles stared back at them. Countless bows were drawn and aimed at them, and somewhere behind them the other ninety were coming down the Z-shaped hall.

"What was it you said last time?" Taunauk asked. The barbarian stood tall, not bothering to ready his axe.

"If everything went to *stercus*? I think it did." She had called it back in the Z-shaped hall. *A good place for an ambush*. But what other choice did they have: Stay in that blasted first room and starve or press forward and be murdered by goblins?

The room they were in was at least a hundred paces in every direction. The center of the room was roughly twenty paces down and surrounded by ringed by stone stairs leading down. The floor in the bottom center looked like a wooden trap door, possibly leading to somewhere—anywhere else.

Four columns rose up in the four corners, all adorned by carved Terrans in a procession. The carvings wrapped around and down the columns, walking to some unseen depths.

Goblins lined the edge of the room, armed with ransacked weapons and armors. Countless bows were aimed at them.

It might have been a decent way to die, had there not been the trap door in the center of the floor. Another chance at escape.

The words of Widewill echoed in her head: *Do not go into the crypt.*

Helesys looked again at the goblins around the room. Most were around the uppermost edge of the room. Some stood on the first set of stairs. None were anywhere near the trap door. Whatever was down there, the goblins would not go near it. Helesys thought that whatever it was it could not be worse than the ambush they found themselves in.

Then a rumbling voice came from above them. From somewhere high in the center of the room. It rumbled, bellowed, in the deepest, most eloquent voice Helesys could imagine.

"You are not welcome here."

Helesys crouched slightly at the voice as she looked up and searched the walls for it. The same feeling came upon her—of being watched by some unseen eye. The elf forced herself to stand tall.

"We had little choice," Helesys said.

"You speak truth," the voice rumbled. "Choose now for a swift death and be gone from my realm."

Taunauk grunted, but the elf could only guess his meaning. Helesys had already chosen her direction. She hoped the barbarian could keep up.

She sprinted forward, down the stairs and toward the trapdoor in the center of the room. Her arm crackled with power and with a quick burst the trapdoor exploded in shards and a rain of planks. A passageway lay under it, leading into darkness.

Helesys slid the final stride and landed in the dark, narrow passageway. She heard the light strides of Taunauk behind her. The two ran into the dim gloom, and only slowed when they were surrounded by blackness.

It was strange. No arrows had been fired. No battle cries or shouts of rage had come from the goblins. The only sound the elf had heard was a quiet, collective gasp.

For her and Taunauk had run away from the goblins and into the crypt.

~ ~ ~

The Crypt

The passageway was winding and uncertain, the opposite of the long stone hallways of the dungeon above. Down here Helesys and Taunauk were in a proper cavern. The walls were jagged stone, the floor unlevel. The surfaces were slick with condensation and the air smelled dank with moss or mold.

Fortunately the world was not completely dark. Thin rays of light shown through cracks in the stone above them, casting an ethereal glow on the passageway. Enough for Helesys to see the vague outline of the walls and floor. Enough for her eyes to play tricks on her.

She wondered briefly if it would've been better to be completely blind in the gloom and quickly struck the thought from her mind. Whatever was down here, whatever held such fear over the goblins, Helesys wanted to see it coming. She wanted a chance to fight.

After all, she had faced fishmen, goblins and a giant hydra. What could be worse than those? And no matter the death, her and Taunauk would just reappear at the start of the dungeon, destined—damned—to continue through some new passageway.

The cave passage was wide enough for her and Taunauk to walk abreast, which brought some comfort to their plight. Though her memories were stricken and Helesys could think of no one else she knew, somehow she felt that of all the choices Taunauk would have been her first to wade with her into dangers unknown.

"I thought you said not to go into the crypt," the barbarian jested. He walked with axe gripped tightly in both hands, ready to meet any danger that should come upon them.

"I know what I said." Helesys kept her wand-arm half bent, humming with anticipation.

Arcane power burned warm in her arm, the barely-contained violence comforting. The full power of it had blown apart one of the heads of the giant hydra, surely it would mean doom for any beast down here. The recoil had been too much to bear, but now Helesys would be ready for it; she was re-learning herself and her power with voracity, and becoming more capable with every encounter.

She thought of Stizzai, the goblin leader, and Helesys vowed she would not be set upon so easily again. No matter what speed or magic armor the goblin brought to bear, Helesys would find a way.

The cavern passage led to one surrounded by stone blocks rather than jagged rocks, as if it was built with the dungeon above it. In this new section, sarcophagi lined the walls. Each lay tucked into an alcove just big enough for one, alcoves arranged in columns of three. For a moment, Helesys found comfort in the familiar geometry of the dungeon but that comfort was quickly forgotten when she saw that the lids to the sarcophagi—all of them—were broken. And empty.

"More undead?" Taunauk asked.

Helesys thought of the flooded temple and the rotting undead that had attacked them. Thought of more of them filling the dark corners of the crypt. They were a dull creature but she had no desire to face so many in such a confined space.

She looked closer at the scene. "I do not think we have to fear them. Look, most pieces are inside the sarcophagus. The lids are broken from the outside as if someone smashed their way in... I can't imagine there are many graverobbers here."

"A scavenger then."

"Likely some ungodly creature."

The barbarian looked at several more sarcophagi and then into the gloom. "Long gone."

"Like the wormsign," Helesys offered, recalling the great passage they had crossed their first time in the dungeon.

Taunauk grunted in reply. "We should not stay here."

"I agree." Helesys spared only a moment longer, looking over the carvings in the stone. The carvings were primitive and crude to the point of being simple and iconic. There were swords and groups of stick-figure men which she could only guess was meant to be an army. But one in particular drew her eye. A pair of wolves, repeated on almost every row.

"We have seen one wolf, three wolves on armor, and now a pair of wolves."

Taunauk grunted impatiently.

Helesys committed it to memory and did not keep him waiting, for she knew the barbarian's sense of danger was keen.

~

The passage of the crypt passed in eerie silence, for even in a crypt empty of the dead Helesys had expected something to set upon them.

After tense minutes, the passage gave way to jagged sides again before opening to a sprawling, contorted cavern—or so it seemed in the darkness. Helesys's eyes adjusted to the room and she saw that it was only forty paces wide but sprawled out over a hundred paces deep. In the distance the thin beams of light from the dungeon above were little more than strands.

"We must not stay here," Taunauk muttered. The barbarian glanced around the cavern, searching for *something*.

"What do you feel?" As soon as the question left her lips, she felt an ominous air drift through the cavern, a cold front that seeped through her skin and into her bones. Something was in here with them. Helesys tucked her metal arm close and called upon its power; one to be ready and second to feel its warmth.

"I feel death unlike anything… Something wicked comes for us. We must not stay here." The barbarian stalked forward through the gloom of the cavern and Helesys followed.

Whatever Taunauk felt, whatever he sensed, rattled him more than the hydra and an agonizing death in its maw. The elf was inclined to trust the human's judgment of such things.

Their careful pace through the cavern did not last. Taunauk's silent feet became long strides and then the two were running across the cavern.

Behind them, Helesys heard the faintest sound of rain on the cavern floor. Steady. Quickening. Coming for them.

They passed thin beam after thin beam of light in the darkness. Ahead of them, the cavern narrowed to a single passage.

Behind them, the rain was moving with the speed of a storm, the pitter patter of drops growing louder—angry.

They would not make it. Her arm whirred violently in anticipation. Helesys turned and met the wicked thing with violence.

"Helesys, no!" the barbarian screamed, but his voice sounded distant—far behind her as she stared at the horror.

In front of the elf, the cavern—entire cavern—squirmed. At first she thought it might have been an ungodly swarm of rats or bats or creeping slime, but it was not.

Helesys leveled her wand, let loose the blast and the purple torrent shot forth into the black creeping thing, illuminating a fraction of their enemy. In the black, covering the floor, walls and ceiling were hands. A squirming, writhing mass. The steady raindrops she had heard were nothing more than thousands of hands crawling in a mass toward her. All were the blue-black color of death. The purple torrent sailed into dozens of hands that clawed their way along the floor, tearing them into black mist that sprayed on their fellows and perturbed none of the others.

"Mother of Movernus," the elf whispered. She backed away, mouth agape as the wicked thing came toward her with the sound of steady rain.

And Taunauk came sailing over her and into the clawing mass.

The pitter patter of the many-handed horror paused for only a moment and the barbarian cried out in rage and surprise and in pain. "Run!" Taunauk screamed and his cry was cut short.

Rage overcame Helesys—rage and desperation. She knew not what the beast was, only that she would not leave her comrade to its dead embrace.

Her wand glowed with a quiet white light. The same it had glowed when translating the speech of the elemental and of the goblins. The sound of the wicked creature was transformed from a quiet summer rain to… screams. Each drop a cry of terror. Overlapping voices—a cacophony of a thousand souls.

"Give him back!" the elf shouted into the frothing black and the glow of her wand-arm grew white hot. The ancient words came back to her, "*Protegentibus lucem.*" Her hand glowed white and the light grew blinding and washed over the cavern, and the uncountable hands recoiled in unison.

A figure flew past her. Taunauk had leapt from the grasp of the creature and landed on his hands and knees. The left side of the barbarian's cloak was ripped in half and revealed a dozen gashes and a mangled arm. Bright red blood poured onto the ground around his hand.

"Get up, barbarian! You will not die here!"

Spurred on by Helesys's words and some deep seated fear, the warrior stumbled down the hall. Helesys followed, burning her arm bright to keep the creature at bay. The translated screams were gone, replaced with the sound of creeping rain as the creature flowed into the passageway after them. The hands grasped the walls, pulling themselves along.

In the bright light she saw even more of the grisly creature: Some hands were no bigger than hers. Others were the size of a child's, but in the center was a giant's hand—big enough to wrap around her shoulders. When it grasped the rock floor, the whole of the creature lurched forward.

"Trapdoor," Taunauk called.

Helesys couldn't look away—dared not look away. The many-handed horror was ten paces away. Seven. Five. Three.

Behind her, the creak of the trapdoor opening. A scrambling of feet and hands on the rock. In front of her, the Horror grew desperate, reaching toward her with the giant, blue-black hand in spite of the light.

Then something picked Helesys up by her robe and she felt cold steel on the back of her neck. Her savior hoisted her out of the trapdoor and hurled her across the room.

~

Helesys rolled across the floor and came to a sprawled stop on the stone.

Taunauk lay on the ground beside her, pushing himself to stand. Blood ran steadily down his left arm from his injuries. Whatever the Horror in the crypt had done to him had been grievous and happened in the span of a second.

Two giant men wearing obsidian-black armor were beside the trapdoor, sliding a heavy beam into the locks. The trapdoor shook violently with the sound of rain, of hundreds of hands battering against it.

The elf reached a metal hand over to her comrade and set it on his back, where the skin was flayed open in deep gashes. "Do not move," she said. The barbarian nodded faintly. Helesys whispered the words and flared her gauntlet, burning it bright as she did to fend off the Horror in the crypt. White light washed over the room and the metal grew burning hot. Taunauk groaned as she cauterized his wounds, but he did not move. Helesys held her breath so as not to smell the burning flesh.

Out of the corner of her eye, she saw the two men in obsidian armor like crisp, black shadows. They let her finish tending to the barbarian. They stood still, five paces away, towering over her, head and shoulders above even Taunauk.

It wasn't until Helesys was done and Taunauk rose to his knee that Helesys took in the full sight of the men. The black metal armor was such a deep color that it seemed to absorb the light from her wand. The armor was bulky and smooth, expertly made and when she looked upon the faces of the giant men, Helesys saw nothing but more metal. Only the inside of the helmet. She looked upon the other joints and saw no skin beneath them. Armor given life. The two metal men stood still even as Helesys stood and Taunauk rose to unsteady feet. On each of their backs was a single, giant warhammer befitting them.

Helesys looked around the room and saw nowhere to run. The room itself was barely thirty paces square. There were two hallways, one which likely led back the way they came, the other further into the dungeon, but neither mattered for dozens of goblins stood in both. They crowded just into the room, clambering to see over each other. The only other way out of the room was the trapdoor that lay ominously in the center; the faintest sound of rain coming from beneath the thin wooden boards.

The room was a prison by any other name.

The rumbling voice of Zhug came from above them, even higher than the animated armor. "Most foolish. Reckless. You bumble about with the innocence of children. As if you do not fear death."

"We do not fear death," Helesys replied, craning her neck to speak to the voice. "We do not fear you."

A deep grumble filled the room—a laugh. "But there are things you should fear, little elf. There are worse fates… But you've got some fight in you and it's been too long since I've tested my creations against a weaver. Survive against them and I'll entertain the thought of letting you both leave my lair."

Two metal men. One for each of them. All Helesys needed to hear was the tightening of Taunauk's hands upon his axe.

Her metal arm was already hot and the arcane torrent burst out easily, like the crack in a dam finally breaking. The purple blast splashed across her target, shimmering like a broken wave on the void-black armor and dissipated like a wave on a rock— the armor didn't so much as falter. It pulled the giant warhammer overhead, then it strode toward her. The sliding and clicking of its armor was overshadowed by Taunauk's roar. The barbarian leapt toward the other armor and met it with a crash of metal.

"*Protegentibus lucem!*" Helesys backed away from her obsidian foe and raised her metal arm in a warding light, just as she'd done with the Horror. White light flooded the room and her arm burned hot, but still the armor strode toward her, black as a silhouette. Whether the warding light was not meant for it or whether it was protected against it she could not guess.

"*Stercus,*" she mumbled, cursing her lack of memory. She ducked under the first swing of the warhammer, the reach so wide that it scraped the stone wall behind her. "You're lucky I do not remember more spells."

She remembered precisely two. The newest was the warding light. The first was the arcane blast—something so primal she remembered it when she had forgotten everything else but her name. So innate that she needed no words to use it. It had come as naturally as breathing, as if her gauntlet was made precisely for it—made for raw, focused power.

Her wand-arm churned with excitement, as if the wand itself were an animal in the middle of a hunt, thrilled with the chase to be used exactly as it was made.

Helesys leveled her arm and let loose a torrent of purple power. This time the suit of armor stuttered in its approach as blast after blast collided with it. Still the metal man swung its warhammer, this time in a diagonal arc that crunched against the stone floor and sent shards scattering. Helesys rolled to the opposite side and felt the vicious wind brush over her head and shoulders.

She saw Taunauk in a mad fury, his battleaxe spinning with galewind speed. Somehow the outlander still fought with his mangled arm and chest. Each blow of the axe showering sparks off the obsidian armor of his foe, but doing nothing. The void-black armor was immaculate, practically spitting in the face of the wounded barbarian.

Helesys's own foe was unscathed as well. Was this how it would end? Barely surviving denizens and horrors only to again face an insurmountable foe. She thought back to the hydra and the fishmen and smiled. If she was going to die again, then she would make it as painful as possible for her foe—if the metal man felt pain at all.

Helesys called upon her arm, drawing deep like the wand was some unfathomable well. She dredged its raw power up, filling the length of her arm and felt the arcane metal workings inside spinning, humming, churning, and finally straining to contain the power. She had blown apart a hydra's head with such a blast. She would do the same to Zhug's metal man.

The power rattled her arm, her collarbone, chest and even the teeth in her skull and still Helesys hung on, fingertips on the edge of a cliff.

The obsidian warrior brought the warhammer around again, preparing to swing and Helesys let go, unleashing the torrent of barely-contained power. A flash of purple and a screech of metal filled the room and for a moment Helesys as blind and deaf to the world.

Except for the pain. Her metal arm was numb and her shoulder and chest were seizing. The elf gasped for air as her heart skipped beat after beat. At some point she had slammed into the stone wall from the recoil, but it was an afterthought to trying to breathe.

A silent world came back into view. Her foe, the giant metal man, still stood. Half its obsidian-black body was dripping, nearly reduced to molten glass. The rest of its armor smoldered with steam as it stared at her with the empty helmet. The top of the warhammer was melting. The smell of molten glass filled the room as the metal man stood facing her, as if contemplating what to do with the elf weaver.

Meanwhile Taunauk had lost his axe and was hanging onto the back of his armored foe. The barbarian began to glow in a faint golden light. Sound finally came back to the world as Taunauk roared and the metal screeched—the barbarian was tearing apart the armor with his bare hands!

Then Helesys's foe reached down to her with a steaming gauntlet. Her eyes went wide and though she scrambled, the pain in her chest had nearly paralyzed her. She felt the heat even before the metal touched her shoulder and then she felt nothing but burning as its near-boiling hand clamped down on her wand-shoulder. The elf let out a pitiful scream and smelled her own flesh. The animated armor picked her up and hurled her across the room like a doll.

But instead of striking stone she struck flesh.

The last thing she heard before she blacked out was the voice of Zhug. "Restrain them both."

~ ~ ~

Kneel

Helesys awoke to the sound of chains and the feeling of swaying—to Taunauk carrying her down a hall. He was cradling her and the elf could feel his wounded arm shaking with the strain beneath her back. In front and behind them were both obsidian metal men, close enough to touch.

Her hands were bound, with a special metal covering locked around her wand-hand, keeping it balled up in a fist. Her feet were bound in chains and from the clinking below her she surmised that her barbarian comrade was too.

She looked up and saw that the human's face was set, jaw clenched. The wounds he sustained at the hands of the Horror spread from his arm and up his shoulder, neck and the side of his face. They were red gashes that seeped blood and were in patterns of four and five—as if the touch of the Horror had melted his skin.

"You can put me down Taunauk," she said.

The barbarian set the elf down without meeting her eye. Helesys realized that she felt much better on the floor, with her feet beneath her. Perhaps her first comment to Taunauk had not been so much out of pride but out of disdain for being off her feet.

'The metal men stopped walking and started again without protest as Helesys walked beside the human. His arm was still shaking, even without the strain of holding her.

"I said you would never have to carry me," Helesys muttered.

Taunauk smiled. "A bane already forgotten. One day you might repay the favor."

Helesys chuckled in spite of the pain it caused her chest. "As long as it is not far." The light air quickly faded when she realized the barbarian was without his axe. "Where is your axe?"

"Back there." He sighed. "I doubt I will need it much longer."

The two shuffled further and further down the long hall— the same worn stone as every other part of the dungeon. The jest of the moment faded and Helesys cursed the stones. She would have damned every single block if she had the time. But before she did, the end of the hall came into view.

It gave way to a magnificent room illuminated bright with torchlight. The green-blue discoloration that marked every other stone in the dungeon gave way to crisp, unmarred white stones that seemed to glimmer in the flickering light. The room stretched out forty paces in either direction, and nearly as high above them. Hanging from the center of the room was a giant chandelier that was nearly as wide as the ceiling.

All around the room were piles of wondrous things: Piles of armor, a giant metal crab big enough for a dozen goblins to fit inside, piles of gold coins, stacks of weapons, mantles of jewelry, bottles with all manner of colors of liquid inside—

some even swirled with smoke. Helesys saw the pattern repeated, the edges of the entire room lined with trinkets and treasures—

—and they all hummed with power. Just as her wand did. Gods, where had it all come from?

And to the left, at the front of the room, sat a giant so big that she thought him a statue until he blinked.

The giant was enormous, nearly twenty paces tall from where it sat comfortably on the stone. Its skin was pale and mottled, with pink muscle and blue veins showing in patches on its arms. It wore a patchwork fur vest and leggings, stitched together from hundreds of different animals. The throne it sat on was broken and wide, and Helesys realized that the beast had likely destroyed the actual throne and merely sat upon the old platform that held it. In its massive left hand it held three magic staffs, one between each finger—though they were made to be two-handed staves for a Terran, for the giant they were little more than wands. If the beast were to stand it might've scraped its crown on the chandelier above them.

Its face was weary, deep creased with pronounced ridges, similar to the goblins that shared the dungeon with it. One eye was bloodshot red, the other a brilliant glass that glowed periodically with light—and magic. Atop its head sat a crown of woven branches.

Even more so than its glass eye, Helesys was drawn to the giant's ears. Uncountable earrings adorned them, but one in particular—only one—was magical. The earring closest to its real eye was adorned with purple jewels and—

—The giant locked eyes with Helesys. It grumbled and waved its wand hand. Helesys felt a pull of some unseen force, yanking her off her feet. It brought her and Taunauk forward, sliding on their knees until they came to a stop in front of the giant.

Taunauk tried to stand but the giant spoke, "I'd prefer you stay there, outlander." It spoke in the same rumbling, floating voice that called itself Zhug. "And you, weaver, keep your metal hand still beneath its confines."

Then Helesys felt the same eerie feeling of being watched from something invisible, something floating around her. Zhug's glass eye glowed with power while she felt the unseen presence.

"Have you been following us this whole time?"

Zhug nodded his massive head.

Suddenly the unseen presence she felt in the dungeon made sense. Zhug had been incorporeal. *Scrying*—the word came back to Helesys from some forgotten arcane knowledge. Zhug's eye was magical and allowed incorporeal sight. A much needed trick for a creature that must have had to crawl through the hallway to his throne room.

"Quite a trick for a giant," Helesys said.

"Remarkably astute for an elf. Slow for a weaver." Zhug grumbled and shifted his enormous bulk. Chips of stone scattered across the floor. "You must be new."

Helesys gritted her teeth at the insult, but curiosity was the stronger force. "What do you know of this place?"

Zhug squinted and bared his teeth. He laughed, a low, thundering rumble that shook the room. And when he was done, he asked, "Why should I help you?"

"One weaver to another."

"Try again."

"We only wish to pass through your realm. We seek to escape this place."

Zhug's toothed smile grew. "And if I told you there is no escape?"

"I would not believe you," the elf replied.

"In my imprisonment I have known many creatures, beings of untold knowledge and power, against the likes of which you pale in comparison. They are trapped, as am I. You are bold, elf. You are bold and this place—this prison—will break you, but I can see this does not dissuade you. Let me offer you a riddle… What happens to you, if I kill you right here on your knees?"

"We would be reborn in some other cursed hall. Just as you would."

The giant nodded. "So what reason do I have to help you when I can simply be rid of you? Send you to someone else's home."

Taunauk spoke wearily, "Eventually you would see us again."

Zhug's smile faded and mirrored the barbarian's. "I might see you again, many deaths from now. Even the strength of an outlander has limits. How many deaths would you endure as you searched for a way out? How many, outlander? Ten? A hundred? Would you die a thousand deaths with no hope of salvation? No. I have seen the depths of despair wrought by this place and *my* strength is no match for it."

"Then help us," Helesys said. "Give us something from your stores, something you would not miss."

At this, Zhug's eyes grew wide and his massive bulk shifted on the stone. He leaned forward, his bulk nearly overwhelming as he towered over them. "Speak plainly, weaver."

Unsure of what had sparked the giant to curiosity or malice, she repeated, "If you must kill us, then give us something to bring back."

Zhug stared at her for a long moment, both his blood red eye and glass scrying eye shifting, examining her. Did he think she was lying—about what?

...About *bringing something back.*

"We brought this back," she said, trying to still the tremble in her voice. As soon as she said it she feared she had made a mistake.

"Show me," Zhug said sternly.

Helesys reached with her chained left hand into the pouch of her robe and pulled out the wolf-plate. The curious engraved disk that she had brought back from her first death.

She held it up for the giant. "We found this in the flooded temple of the fishmen. I died with it in my pocket and when I was reborn it was still in my pocket."

The elf wondered if the giant would inspect it, or simply take it and toss it amongst his horde of treasure, but he did neither. Zhug leaned back, his bulk crunching stone as he did, and pondered what she said for a long moment.

Finally Zhug asked, "What are your names?"

"Helesys," the elf replied, leaving out her family name of Byyra. The omission was forgotten within a flicker of torchlight.

"Taunauk."

The giant nodded thoughtfully. "Helesys and Taunauk, the claim you make is no small one and it changes things considerably."

"Have you heard the likes of it before?" she asked.

"This prison is far older than I and far larger than my realm. I have heard of such things but only in speculation. Only in myths that offer hope of change. But you stand before me, clearly. As does your proof."

"Do you have wisdom for us?" Taunauk asked. The barbarian spoked forcibly, though Helesys could see that even on his knees he was swaying. Losing strength.

Zhug held up three massive fingers of his free hand and lowered one at a time as he spoke. "You must steel yourself for if your journey is far, far from over. As your memories come back, you must not forget the person you have created in this place. Last, as a blessing, I will allow you each to take one treasure of mine with you. You may rise."

Both Helesys and Taunauk stood, though the barbarian did so with difficulty. The weight of the chains and the clamp on her wand-arm pulled on her shoulders as the elf stood, sending sharp pain through her shoulder and chest.

The beautiful voice of a female elf echoed through her head, a memory she did not recognize: *Power has no limits, but the body does.*

Zhug swept a free hand over the room, bidding them to pick something, but Helesys was more curious about the giant than she was about the treasures surrounding them.

"Why are you helping us?" she asked.

"Calculated interest. Choose a blessing," Zhug rumbled impatiently.

Helesys and Taunauk walked around the room together. She slowed to his pace. The two obsidian metal men followed them with gentle steps and gentle clicks of their armor.

All the while the giant behind her was not forgotten. Again she felt Zhug scrying over her shoulder. She turned back to see him watching, his magic eye glowing with power. Did he watch out of mistrust or curiosity? Perhaps both.

As they walked, Helesys took in the sights of the treasure room. There were so many intricate pieces and yet, now that she was closer to them, she could feel the pulls of the magic within them. Each one tugging at her attention. Helesys was reminded of the feeling of using her wand—yearning to be used. The magic within each artifact was a tool, idle and languishing, desperate for purpose.

She passed frost-covered boots, a staff with silver patterns of dragons and fire, a shimmering cloak the color of a night sky, and tomes bound in metal sheets, oak, and skin. She passed armor and weapons that hummed with power much like her arm, forces that turned one warrior into ten. She passed potions that glowed and shimmered and churned all while their bottles stayed still.

Each called to her, whispering promises of power, of secret histories long forgotten. Yet the elf weaver passed all these things, knowing that each would be a boon unto itself. She passed all these things without knowing why.

"It is impossible to choose," she said quietly.

"An impossible choice for an impossible place," Zhug grumbled from his throne. So he had been listening as much as watching through his scrying eye.

Then Helesys came to a pile of gold and jewels nearly as tall as she and she stopped cold. It was not the riches nor the colors that dotted the pile that called to her. Something buried inside called to her with a quiet voice. Something meek and easily forgotten amidst the treasure horde.

Helesys reached into the pile, sliding gold coins in broad pushes, layer after layer. She heard the crunch of the shifting giant atop his throne. Something hidden in the pile, something he hadn't counted on her to find.

Then she saw it: A single gold coin. Helesys regarded it as if it was a poisonous spider, for the word it whispered to her was *death*. She snatched it quickly. Then picked up another coin in her elven hand and regarded them both. They were exactly the same. They both had the face of some long forgotten ruler stamped on one side and a wolf's head on the other.

The wolf's head gave her pause, but the question was soon forgotten.

"I want this coin," Helesys declared, turning back toward Zhug. The giant was leaning forward on his throne with a face of surprise. His staves were pointed lazily in her direction. "What is this?"

Zhug leaned back on his throne before answering. He rapped fingers on the stone, the impact echoing through the room. All the while his staves never moved away from her.

The giant's eyes were harsh. "A coin stained with the blood of a murdered weaver: A magekiller token. It will allow you to more easily cut through the defenses of a mage and more easily bear their offences. Do not let it give you ideas in my realm," the giant added sternly, "for its magic is a cheap thing and one easily countered by those of knowledge and prowess."

Helesys smirked in spite of the grim proclamation. "Do not fear, Zhug."

"I do not."

Both their eyes were drawn to Taunauk as the mangled barbarian hoisted a large darkwood shield from the floor. He hoisted it and felt its weight before declaring, "I shall have this."

"That is an ironwood shield," Zhug said. "Ironwood is stronger than steel but only when kept in sheets of bark. As such, it can never be fashioned into a weapon."

"Not even saplings?" Taunauk asked.

At that the giant smirked. "Saplings my size are not mature enough to be used as clubs. The shield you hold is one of the only Ironwood pieces I have seen in this realm. In the out-lander tongue it is called *Foghar siorruidh.* In the common tongue—"

"—*Everfall*," the barbarian replied, spellbound. As if the shield had helped rekindle some bid of knowledge or language.

"Yes," Zhug replied.

Meanwhile, Helesys felt the quiet whisper of the magekiller token. Without thinking, she slipped it into a groove of her gauntlet. She felt gears of her arm slipping and changing, modeling themselves anew—incorporating the token into the arcane channels of power. The whispers of the token stopped.

Zhug had not been pleased at her choice, but then Helesys would not have been either to see a possible rival choose a boon that would make them a stronger enemy.

~

They had made their choice.

"Now it is time for you to die," Zhug grumbled.

Helesys looked to Taunauk and saw the defeat on his face. The barbarian did not even raise his shield. Everfall hung at his side. She could not even unclasp her wand-hand to fire one last time.

"All that just to kill us anyway?"

Zhug nodded. "Because I have known your kind: Adventurers, ratcatchers, knight errants—damned fools, all—and not to be trusted. I've fought and killed the lot of them. I mean what I say, I will kill you and be rid of you. You will be a plague upon someone else's house."

The giant leaned forward, pointing the three staves at them, "I ask one thing in return for a swift death—"

"One death is no different from another," Taunauk groaned.

"Ah, but you are wrong, outlander. There are gods trapped here… and then there are things within these walls that even those gods fear. One lives in my crypt." The giant's red eye grew wide with excitement. "Do you know what would have happened to you, had you perished by the many hands of Shomosk? It would have counted an outlander's hands among its collection and the weaver would go on the rest of her days here alone."

Taunauk said nothing, but bowed his head.

Helesys regarded her comrade, but turned back to the giant. "How can we know which deaths are preferable and which to avoid?"

The giant's one red eye rolled back in thought. "Here the cycle of death and rebirth burns fast, like a bonfire doused with ether—neverending. But there are *lingering* deaths: The desperate hands of Shomosk, the rotting undead, the parasite… You will know them when you see them."

Helesys nearly scoffed, but the memory of the crypt was fresh in her mind. She thought back to the Many-Handed Horror, Shomosk, and the utter revulsion and despair, the desperate need to get away.

"A swift death is preferable," the elf said. "Name your price."

"If you die a thousand deaths and find yourselves in my halls again... If you find yourself set against me and hold my life in your hands... Grant me mercy."

Helesys regarded the giant, wondering both why he would fear them and why he would fear death. She nodded and the human grunted in reply.

Zhug pointed the wand at Helesys and it crackled with deep greens and blacks. "A thousand deaths to you both. *Somnum mortis.*"

The last thing she saw was the stoic face of the giant. The last thing she felt was that the words were a blessing.

~ ~ ~

Second Death

Blackness. Silence. Peace.

Then she was falling.

Helesys landed and crouched to a roll on the stone. Taunauk landed beside her, catching himself with strength and without flair. His wounds were completely healed, his cloak and leather armor untorn. The Everfall shield upon his back. The image of him nearly dead, nearly trapped within Shomosk lingered in her mind; it would not easily be forgotten.

The pair stood wearily in the starting room. The innocuous stone and line of torches on the wall that marked a death and rebirth. Was Zhug right? Ten deaths would wear on them. A hundred would destroy them. More than that was unthinkable.

The Outlander walked to examine the line of torches on the wall and the elf watched him. "You knew the danger when we were in the crypt… Why did you do it? Why did you sacrifice yourself for me? Is it some kind of misguided, human code?"

Taunauk ran his hand over the stone and shook his head. "You are my friend." He walked the length of the torch-wall and back again. She did not fill the silence, so the outlander did. "It is not my nature to let my friends die." Taunauk shook his head in frustration. "I know not whether it is by nature or clan or by oath, but I will not watch you die again. Do not ask this of me."

Helesys stared at the barbarian, a human she counted as her comrade—her only friend—and felt a sadness that she could barely understand and that she would not show. She had found the limits of an outlander. A warrior with strength most mortals could not comprehend, who fought monsters and creatures unspeakable and who was not afraid to perish at their hands... but who could not *share* the burden of watching a friend die.

"I will not ask it of you," she replied. She would shoulder that burden alone.

Taunauk nodded and the man with shoulders of a mountain walked back and pulled a torch from the wall. Stone scattered across the room.

She looked upon the outlander and dwelled on the thought: Just who had they been? A stoic warrior with some sense of honor. An elven spellslinger to whom violence came all too easily. Would they simply *become* again? Reclaim their old memories and their old ways to become their former selves?

Something inside her whispered, *no*. There were many curses heaped upon her and Taunauk, but there was one blessing among them: Perspective. She could look upon herself anew and, like a craftsman, decide which elements to keep, which to reforge, and which to cast aside. In spite of this vow,

Helesys sensed that some things, namely violence, would be hard to reforge. But there were things she could start with.

"My name is Helesys Byyra," she said, telling her comrade the family name. One thing she had omitted in the flooded temple. She decided it was a reservation unfounded.

The barbarian looked to her and smiled a candle's warmth. "I am Taunauk of clan Aonar." Then he turned and walked to the hallway—to uncertainty and to change. To the unknown. Helesys followed behind.

Why shouldn't she share the snippets of past that she recalled? After all, her and Taunauk were bound by something, something that felt stronger than chance. There had to be a reason that they both wound up here together. Time after time.

She had agreed to the outlander's terms without debate, just as she had agreed to Zhug's terms. As if pity for a friend and the threat of a lingering death were enough. Worse, she still had questions. And they were no closer to escape, something that eluded even Zhug with his knowledge, treasure and untold years here.

Zhug had called this place a prison—a dungeon by any other name. She'd been right about this cursed place after all.

But they were different. Zhug's surprise at that fact had not escaped the elf. When others died they did not bring back treasures such as her and Taunauk had. She had no idea what it meant and it was a small comfort as they reached the edge of the hall. With each death they would learn, they would bring back weapons and treasure. Their power would grow. In time, they would be rid of this place.

The weaver and barbarian paused only a moment at the entryway for only a moment. Taunauk said quietly, "I will go first."

~ ~ ~

NEXT TIME ON
A BATTLEAXE AND
A METAL ARM
Book 3:

The Forest and the

Infinite Wall
Available June 2021

Spoiler–Free excerpt from *BAMA 3*

Taunauk did not ask further and offered a hand to pull the weaver up. Helesys looked out over the death and destruction she had wrought in the forest and felt somber. Somber that it had been so easy, in spite of the blowback she had felt, and somber that the surrounding trees—the dungeon itself—was unaffected by such power.

"Do you see… What is that?" the barbarian asked. He pointed out with the blade of his axe, gesturing to a building deep in the forest. They might have walked past it if not for the woodsmen, yet it was only visible now that they had been reduced to ash.

"Let's see what we've uncovered," the weaver said.

The ruin of the woodsmen extended hundreds of feet into the forest. The pair walked through ash and broken dryads all the way to the ancient structure.

It was made from the same thick gray stone as the dungeon and was about two stories tall, mirroring the parapets of the dungeon on a much smaller scale. The part that was still standing might have been fifty paces square. The two windows Helesys could see were dark and showed no light from the inside.

Helesys looked back between the structure and the road and saw the occasional rock surface from beneath the sparse grass—perhaps remnants. Whatever the stone building had been, now it was half-destroyed.

As Helesys and Taunauk carefully rounded a corner, they saw small outcroppings of bark and vine arranged in a circle about a clearing. The outer edge bore similarities to the woodsmen in stature and figure, but they did not move at all. As Helesys looked inward at the circle she saw the figures shrink in stature and she realized that they were growing from the center of the clearing.

And in the center of the clearing and growth, she saw two statues in the grass. They saw the back of a kneeling soldier, the outline of a helm and shoulder pauldrons beneath a covering of green moss. In front of it, they saw the towering statue of a maiden, as tall as the gatehouse. In contrast, her stone was pearl-grey and no moss touched any of her.

Then the knight-statue stood up and calmly turned to face them.

There was a woman's face beneath the plate armor, seemingly half Terran and half woodsman, her armor a blend of steel and bark and moss. Her eyes were the color of moss and her left cheek was a sheet of bark.

"Long ago there was a Gatekeeper who lived here," the green knight said. Her voice was melodic as a song and carried a breeze with it. "She was raven-haired and fair. Ungodly beautiful and equally kind. She wanted for one thing, for someone to share her warmth... She waited long.

"I have never seen her again. I suspect they are somewhere in the castle walls, numb to the kingdom that has grown in their stead. This statue is all I have left of her."

"Perhaps they would know how to escape this place?" Helesys asked.

The knight stared back in confusion. "Death is the only escape."

"No. I mean escape from this prison, this dungeon… Back to the real world."

"I do not understand. Are there not stars in the sky? Do you not feel pain and warmth and loss and breath?"

"You will wait here with me for the Gatekeeper's return." Wind whipped around the trees as she spoke. "You are in need of faith."

Helesys's wand-arm churned with power. She glanced at Taunauk and saw his chest heave in a sigh.

To be continued June 2021

Thank you for Reading

I hope you enjoyed reading this story as much as I enjoyed writing it.

If you did, I would massively appreciate a short review on Amazon or your favorite book website. Reviews are crucial for any author, and a starred review or even just a line or two can make a huge difference.

It's especially true for the start of a series. Thanks and I hope you enjoy the next one!

<u>For a limited time</u>: Sign up for Sam's *Monthly Newsletter* and get Free Phone and Desktop Backgrounds featuring art from *A Battleaxe and a Metal Arm*! Go to SamuelFlemingBooks.com to sign up, get some free digital art, and keep up with publishing and sales alerts.

Looking for more Bite-Sized Fantasy?

You might like **Tales from Another World, Volume 1**. The first installment contains stories about an undead sorcerer, a druid grove under attack, strange mermaids, a possessed church, a witch sentenced to burn, and commoners caught in-between.

The compilation contains the following stories ranging from 1,000 word short fiction to 5,000 word short stories:

1) The Final Ritual of Sircius Everdeath
2) Under the Waters of Digsonee Strait
3) On the Crimes of Hexing and Bewitchment
4) A Final Plea upon Still Waters
5) The Crypt of St. Lillian
6) The Blessing of the Autumn Herald
7) City of Embers

What to expect in

A Battleaxe and a Metal Arm

I usually save this space for an "On Writing the story" section, but let's do things differently this time. So, what can you expect from this series?

1) You can expect a heaping dose of action, both of the battleaxe and magical prosthetic arm variety.
2) Expect to slowly learn more about Helesys and Taunauk as their memories come back.
3) Expect to learn more about the dungeon as our heroes explore its far reaches.
4) Lastly, you can expect a new story in the series every month. *Sword and Sorcery on a Schedule.*

I thought about going for a story every 2-3 weeks, but I wouldn't be able to keep that pace. I'd rather be consistent.

If you're interested, don't forget to check out the preorder link.

Connect with the Author

If you want to stay up to date on the latest about Samuel's publishing news and blog, check out his website and consider signing up for his monthly newsletter.

www.SamuelFlemingBooks.com

Samuel can also be found on Reddit, Goodreads and Facebook.

Samuel Fleming is a Science Fiction and Fantasy author.

He grew up in Maryland, spending most of his time swimming and writing. Swimming gave him a lot of time to daydream, so the two hobbies complemented each other well. Idle dray dreams turned into stories, some of which stuck with him for years. These days he swims a little less and writes a lot more.

He loves a good story no matter the medium: Books, TV, video games, comics, tabletop RPG's, or podcasts–most of which he attempts to share with his wife and three kids, and occasionally on his blog.